Angelina
and the Rag Doll

Story adapted by KATHARINE HOLABIRD from the TV episode
written by James Mason

BASED ON THE CLASSIC PICTURE BOOKS
BY KATHARINE HOLABIRD AND HELEN CRAIG

E
HOL

PLEASANT
COMPANY
PUBLICATIONS™

Published by Pleasant Company Publications
First published in Great Britain by Penguin Books Ltd., 2002
© 2002 HIT Entertainment PLC
Based on the illustrations by Helen Craig and the text by Katharine Holabird

Visit our Web site at www.americangirl.com
and Angelina's very own site at www.angelinaballerina.com

Manufactured in Hong Kong.
02 03 04 05 06 07 08 09 C&C 10 9 8 7 6 5 4 3 2 1

First Pleasant Company printing, 2002

Library of Congress Cataloging-in-Publication Data
Holabird, Katharine
Angelina and the rag doll / story adapted by Katharine Holabird from the CiTV episode written by James Mason.
p. cm.
"Based on the classic picture books by Katharine Holabird and Helen Craig."
"An Angelina ballerina storybook."
Summary: When Miss Lilly asks Angelina the mouse to be a helper in the beginner ballet class,
Angelina feels very grown-up and decides to give up her babyish rag doll, with unexpected results.
ISBN 1-58485-617-3
[1. Mice—Fiction. 2. Dolls—Fiction. 3. Ballet dancing—Fiction. 4. Growth—Fiction.] I. Mason, James. II. Craig, Helen, ill. III. Title.

PZ7.H689 Alj 2002
[E]—dc21   2001059814

Angelina couldn't wait to tell her best friend, Alice, the exciting news.

"Miss Lilly needs a helper for the beginner's ballet class," Angelina announced proudly as they walked home together, "and she asked ME!"

The two little mouselings went to Mrs. Thimble's General Store to buy some sweets to celebrate.

"Don't forget my secondhand box," Mrs. Thimble reminded them as they were about to leave. "Just bring anything you don't need anymore, and it will help a good cause."

When she got home, Angelina made a collection of all the things she'd outgrown.

"What's this?" asked Alice, holding up an old rag doll mouse in a torn tutu.

"Oh, that's Polka," said Angelina. "We used to dance together when I first started at Miss Lilly's Ballet School."

"Where did you get her?" Alice asked.

"I don't remember," said Angelina. "But I'm too grown-up for her now."

Angelina added Polka to the collection, and the next morning the two mouselings carried all Angelina's old clothes and toys to the General Store, and everything went straight into Mrs. Thimble's secondhand box.

The following week, Angelina's grandpa and grandma came for tea and decided to have a look at Angelina's baby photographs. "Ahh," said Grandma, smiling. "Here's a picture of you at your first ballet lesson, with Polka."

"Do you remember the day I won Polka for you at the fair?" Grandpa asked. "And you said you'd never ever let her go."

"Y-y-yes, Grandpa," Angelina stammered, suddenly remembering.

"You called her Polka because that was the special dance we always did together," Grandpa said. "Let's see if we can still remember it."

But Angelina was already running out the door. "I'm sorry," Angelina called, "but I forgot to tell Alice something important!"

Angelina ran all the way to Alice's cottage to tell her the terrible news.

"We've got to get Polka back!" Angelina shouted. They raced off together as fast as they could to Mrs. Thimble's General Store.

The two mouselings searched in all Mrs. Thimble's secondhand boxes, but Polka was nowhere to be found.

"I'm afraid your doll's already been taken," Mrs. Thimble said.

Angelina couldn't believe that Polka was gone. She made big posters with Polka's picture on them and stuck them all around the village. But nobody brought Polka back.

Then Angelina went up and down the streets with Alice and asked about Polka at every shop and house, but the villagers just shook their heads.

Finally, Angelina and Alice went to see Miss Twitchett, who collected things for charity.

"I've just sent all the toys to the poor children in Dacovia," Miss Twitchett said.

"What am I going to do?" Angelina cried.

"At least you'll have fun helping Miss Lilly at ballet school tomorrow," Alice kindly reminded her.

Angelina couldn't let Miss Lilly down, so the next morning she put on her tutu and went to help with the ballet lessons.

All the little dancers were happily crowding around Miss Lilly, but one small mouseling was too shy to join in.

"Come in and sit down, Mary," said Miss Lilly, smiling. But Mary shook her head and stayed by herself in the corner, clutching an old rag doll.

Angelina looked closer—and gasped. She couldn't believe her eyes—little Mary was holding Polka!

"Excuse me, she's my . . ." Angelina stopped herself. She could see that Mary really loved Polka.

"She's a lovely doll," Angelina said with a smile. "And she loves to dance. May I show you?" Mary nodded and handed Polka to Angelina.

Angelina began to dance with Polka, the way she always used to, and little Mary smiled and forgot about feeling so shy. Soon she was laughing and dancing around and around the room with Angelina and Polka.

"Well done, darlings." Miss Lilly clapped her hands.

For the rest of the lesson, Mary followed Angelina and tried to do all the ballet exercises just the way Angelina showed her.

At the end of the morning, Angelina waited with Miss Lilly to say good-bye to all the new ballet students.

"See you next week, Mary," said Angelina.

"I hope I can be a beautiful dancer like you someday," said Mary, smiling.

"I'm sure you will," Angelina encouraged her.

Mary hugged Polka. "I'm going to call her Angelina. Is that all right?"

"Yes," said Angelina quietly. "I'd really like that."

The next time that Grandma and Grandpa came to tea, Angelina told them all about Polka and Mary.

"I loved Polka, and I'm really sorry for breaking my promise to you, Grandpa," Angelina said.

"You did a very grown-up thing," said Grandpa. "I'm really proud of you, Angelina."

Angelina gave her grandpa an enormous hug, and Mr. Mouseling started to play his fiddle.

"May I have the honor of this dance?" asked Grandpa with a bow.

Angelina curtsied. Then she and Grandpa laughed and danced around the cottage while her father played the polka, and Angelina was absolutely delighted because she still remembered every step!